**Also by the same author,
and available in Knight Books:**

THE HEADMASTER WENT SPLAT!
THE SCOURGE OF THE DINNER LADIES

A Twerp Mystery

The Case of the Feeble Weeble

David Tinkler

**Illustrated
by Gary Andrews**

KNIGHT BOOKS
Hodder and Stoughton

British Library C.I.P.

Tinkler, David
  The case of the feeble weeble
  I. Title II. Andrews, Gary III. Series
  823'.914[J]

ISBN 0 340 52094 9

Printed and bound in Great Britain
for Hodder and Stoughton Children's
books, a division of Hodder and
Stoughton Ltd., Mill Road, Dunton
Green, Sevenoaks, Kent TN13 2YA.
(Editorial Office: 47 Bedford Square,
London WC1B 3DP) by Cox & Wyman
Ltd., Reading, Berks.

I

Maybe you've never ever read anything about the Twerps before and this is the first you have ever heard of them. If so, think VERY CAREFULLY about going on with this book, because reading about the Twerps can be a VERY nasty experience.

Yes.

Certainly.

You could be scarred for life!

Many kind, well-meaning people believe that books about the Twerps should be banned because of the school they go to. It is a terrible school. . .where terror and fear cast grim shadows!

Think about your own dear school. Is it shabby and in need of a lick of paint? Does it smell of dinners and toilets and cheesy feet? Are the teachers a bane and a pain?

Well, Shambles School is EVEN WORSE! However mad and bad your head teacher may be, he or she is *meek* and *mild* compared with Killer Keast.

The Killer has three moods:

His WILD mood.

His SAVAGE mood.

His Grade Z Killer mood.

When he is in his Grade Z mood dark clouds roll overhead and a deadly chill descends upon Shambles School. That's what it was like one November afternoon.

Dark.

Cold.

Silent—Yes, it was silent apart from a chattering noise. That was Mr Weeble's teeth chattering; even the teachers were terrified.

'Weeble!' cried Mr Keast glaring at him from behind his desk.

'Y-yes, sir,' stammered Weeble.

'Stop that blasted chattering!'

'I-I can't help it, sir.'

'Of course, you can! Take them out!'

'Take what out?'

'Your teeth!'

'Oh, yes, sir. Very good idea, sir. Thank you for suggesting it, sir.'

Mr Weeble slipped his false teeth out and put them in his pocket.

After that the chattering stopped.

'Well,' growled Mr Keast. 'What have you come to see me about?'

'You—er—sent for me, sir.'

The Killer glared grimly at the Feeble Weeble: why had he sent for such a drip?

'Ah, yes!' he remembered. 'It's about your job.'

Mr Weeble went deadly pale; was the Killer going to sack him? 'Yes?' he gulped.

'You're Head of Chalk, aren't you?'

Mr Weeble nodded. Actually he was only Head of

Crayons—the lowest teaching job in the school—but he didn't dare contradict the Head in his Grade Z mood.

'Well, Weeble, you may have heard that Mrs Yapp has been taken to the Dunyellin Rest Home. I understand she will be there for some time; apparently she thinks she's a cold hot-water-bottle.'

Mr Weeble nodded gravely.

'So I'm looking for someone to take over her job as Head of Video.'

Mr Weeble beamed; it was a big jump from Head of Crayons to Head of Video. Being Head of Video meant you had a comfy little lair to sit in watching videos. Also more cash. And cash comes in handy.

'Of course you'd only be *Acting* Head of Video,' explained the Killer.

'Acting?' gulped the Weeble. He wasn't very good at acting—far too shy.

'I mean you will only be Head of Video until the end of term. If you do well, then you can keep the job. But if you make a mess of it—then you go back to being Head of Chalk—and if you make an utter, absolute muck up of it, you'll be sacked.'

'Yes, Headmaster. Thank you.'

2

'Did you see old Weeble?' asked Kevin Twerp at teatime. He wasn't actually drinking as he spoke, but his mug was right in front of his mouth so the words came out a bit muffled. Like this: 'Do see o eeble?'

'Wha?' replied Micky Twerp. *Wha?* means *what?* as I expect you realise. It's what happens to the word *what* when you say it with your mouth full of bread and cheese; this eerie sound—wha—comes out of your mouth along with little wet splats of bread.

The little wet splats of bread spray out and hit people in the eye; they never seem to like it.

'Good grief!' cried the boys' mum. 'It's like a chim-panzees' tea-party. Honestly I could charge people to come and look at you! Hercules!'

'Yes?'

'Get your fingers out of the honey! You've just been picking your nose!'

'No I haven't!' cried the little chap indignantly. 'I was just scratching its *inside*!'

'It's like being down on the farm,' sighed Mrs Twerp. 'I think I'll get a trough. Save washing up plates!'

'Wuugh! Wuugh!'—that was Micky Twerp laugh-ing. He always laughed like that.

'It's the way we've been brought up, Flea,' he chort-led.

The three boys called their mum Flea because she was small and jumped about a lot.

'Nonsense!' cried the Flea. 'It's the malignant influence of that dreadful school!'

'Did you see old Weeble?' asked Kevin again. He was looking at Micky when he asked that because, of course, Micky went to Shambles School as well.

'See old Weeble doing what?' asked Micky.

'Grinning without his teeth.'

'Wuugh!'

'Yes,' continued Kevin calmly, 'he was grinning and beaming and skipping about. All because he's been made Head of Video.'

'Head of Video?' squawked the Flea.

'Yeh,' explained Kevin, 'in charge of all the video machines and stuff. He's got to record all the prog-rammes the other teachers want so they can make us sit an' watch them instead of having to teach us themselves.'

'What!' chortled Micky. 'He'll get them all wrong!'

'Yeh!'

'Instead of *Middle School English* it'll be *The Benny Hill Show!*'

'. . .And instead of *Aspects of the Industrial Revolution* it'll be *Top of the Pops!*'

'Yeh!'

'Yeh! Some really boring teacher—like Deathbreath Parkinson—will be there saying, "We will now watch a video showing hydrogen molecules being intensely boring"—and he'll switch on an' it'll be the *EastEnders* being intensely boring instead!'

Wuugh!

Honk!

Splat!

The Flea was sitting on a bean bag well out of range of flying splat. She had her special mug in her hand, the one Hercules had given her for her birthday, and she was gazing over the edge of this mug with a startled expression. Something had surprised her, and it was not the disgusting table manners of her three wild sons.

'Sh!' she suddenly hissed. 'Look!'

'What?' asked Micky.

'Out in the garden—one of the trees—it—it's WALKING TOWARDS THE HOUSE!'

The three boys turned and stared. Then—*Crash*—they crashed and stampeded to the window: three noses (one completely snot-free) pressed against the cold glass.

'I don't believe it,' gasped Micky, 'this CAN'T BE REAL!'

The tree came tottering over the grass towards them. It seemed to be able to *sense* that they were there.

'Maybe it's an alien life form,' murmured Kevin. 'Maybe on some other planets trees have evolved into super-trees.'

Nobody answered this remark.

Then the tree shouted at them.

3

AYLGERRUM! AYLGERRUM! AYLGERRUM!

That was what the tree sounded like. Then, as it came nearer, it started to sound like this:

'I'll get 'em!'

'I'll get 'em!'

'I'll get 'em for this! I'll *pulverise* 'em! I'll. . . .'

'It's Rose,' yelped the Flea.

'What's she doing in a tree?' gasped Micky.

'Rose!' they roared.

'Help!' replied the tree.

The Twerps charged out of the breakfast room and into the conservatory; they bounced through the conservatory leaping nimbly over the bikes and the heaps of toys. Flea got caught up in the Scalextric track—but that didn't hold her up for long—crashing and bashing they rushed out of the conservatory and onto the grass.

The tree had stopped tottering about. In fact it looked just like an ordinary tree apart from having eyes. Yes. It had two eye-sized holes in it and there were these angry eyes looking out of them.

'Rose! Is that you in there?'

'Yes,' replied a muffled voice. 'Help me get out of this ghastly thing—I'm stuck!'

If Rose had been small and skinny and covered in oil, it might have been easier to get her out. But she wasn't. No. Rose was enormous; she was the biggest policewoman in the history of the universe. She rippled and bulged with flesh; the ground shook when she walked.

'Maybe we should squirt washing-up liquid up the tree to make her slippery,' suggested Kevin helpfully.

'We could tie a rope round her ankles and tie the other end to the car and pull her out,' said Micky.

'Just leave her for a day or two without food,' mused the Flea. 'Then she'd lose weight and it'd come off easily.'

'Look, it's made of fibre-glass,' Kevin pointed out. 'Do you think it'd *expand* if we heated it up?'

'*Don't* heat it up!' shrieked Rose. 'Just put it on its side—*gently*—and give my legs a yank.'

'Okay.'

'Wait!' shrieked Rose. 'Don't just shove me over. . . .'

Thud!

That was the *dull thud* that the tree made when it hit the grass. Some of the fibre-glass twigs snapped. Rose had screamed while it was falling and she moaned a bit after the thud.

'Shut up, Rose,' cried the Flea. 'Remember you're a HEROINE with a MEDAL and stop snivelling.'

'I'm not snivelling,' replied Rose with dignity. Then she concentrated on not moaning or groaning or wailing or even going *Ouch*! Because, of course, it

14

was true about her having a medal and people with medals have to be extra brave—even when a family of Twerps is practically pulling their legs off.

'Who put you in that extraordinary thing?' the Flea demanded to know. Rose, who was slumped in an armchair swigging a mug of tea, did not reply immediately. Instead she muttered grimly to herself—something about *getting even* and *they'll be sorry.*

'Well?' asked Flea.

'That tree-suit, Flea, is a *disguise,* ' explained Rose.

'Well, yes, we had actually figured that out for ourselves,' sniggered the Flea. 'We didn't think you'd got it off the peg at Dorothy Perkins! What we want to know is why you were wandering about in it.'

'It's top secret,' answered Rose, 'so I'm afraid I can't tell you about it.'

'About what?'

'About how those sub-human fiends ordered me to get into that ghastly tree-suit and. . . .'

'What!' squeaked the Flea. 'You mean some criminal gang made you wear it?'

'Worse!'

'Worse?'

'Far worse! It was not a criminal gang. It was a pack of madmen—the SERIOUS CRIME SQUAD!'

'What? You mean they were detectives?'

'Exactly!'

'Fiends?'

'*Sub-human* fiends, Flea. But just wait till I get back to the station! I-I'll . . . .'

The Twerp boys were sitting on the bean bags listening to all this. They knew it would be deeply foolish to say anything—or even cough or belch—because whenever Rose was explaining anything TOP SECRET she'd suddenly shut up if she realised the boys were there. She seemed to have this odd idea that top secret police matters were not for young ears.

'The Serious Crime Squad,' explained Rose, 'is a bunch of big-heads from Scotland Yard. They've come muscling in on our patch ordering everyone about because this video gang is in the area. . . .'

'Video gang?'

'Yes. A cunning gang that goes about nicking videos. That's all. Only they broke into Scotland Yard and nicked the videos they use to record *Match of the Day* so, naturally, the big-wigs at the Yard are all steamed up. So, when we started getting a lot of videos being nicked out here, the Yard got all excited and sent this Serious Crime Squad out to catch them. So they're in charge and, instead of letting us get on with things in our own way they keep coming up with daft ideas and, Flea, they made me dress up in that tree and go on surveillance. I've been standing stock still in that blasted tree since breakfast time. And, honestly, the trouble I've had from dogs. I'll have to burn these shoes!'

'Poor Rose.'

'What makes it worse, Flea, is to think that the video-thieves are roaming about our patch and we are *powerless* to catch them because of these idiots telling us what to do!'

'Powerless, Rose?'

'Yes, Flea, *powerless!* I doubt if there'll be a video left in this area by the time they've finished!'

4

Miss Mist, the deeply sensitive Head of Poetry, lived with her cats in an attic close to the school. Often, when she went out, she'd take a short cut through the grounds and think how peaceful everything was and how the whole place seemed to be resting. Now Miss Mist belonged to a special committee of people who were dedicated to bringing art and culture to the Shambles area and, because this was such a *very* difficult task, the meetings always took a *very* long time, so, whenever she went to one, she came home late and took the short cut through the school in the dark. That's what happened on the night after Mr Weeble had been made Acting Head of Video.

She was just walking dreamily though the playground listening to the romantic, scuttling sound of empty crisp packets being blown about in the dark, when she heard a man's voice.

'Is that you?' it asked.

Miss Mist stopped walking and thought about this. She knew the answer, of course, but ladies walking alone in the dark are a bit wary. The voice continued:

'Is that you, Millicent? It's me—William—I'm looking for the light switch.' There was a fumbling noise followed by a click, then a row of outside lights came on and she recognised the tubby shape and smiling face of William Weeble.

'I've got to go in and do some videoing,' he explained.

'So this is where the video hut is,' hissed little Miss Mist. 'I'd always wondered where it was, but being Head of Poetry, I've never used video. You see, William, I have my own special poetry-reading voice and my own special poetry face, so I'd rather read poems myself.'

'Very sensible,' replied Weeble. (He'd thought of saying, 'Very sensible, *my darling*,' but decided not to.)

'But, William,' whispered little Miss Mist (she'd thought of saying, 'But William, *my love*,' but was too shy). 'But, William,' she whispered, 'are you sure you know how to work the machines? Aren't they very complicated?'

'That's the trouble,' sighed the new Head of Video. 'I've no idea how they work. I've got Mrs Yapp's little note-book with a list of programmes to be recorded. But some of them are at the most *peculiar* times—like three o'clock in the morning!'

'Oh,' gulped Miss Mist, 'no wonder Mrs Yapp went mad.'

'I think there's some special way of setting them to go on by themselves but I'd feel foolish asking anyone about it. I mean, imagine what people would think, the Head of Video not knowing what buttons to press!'

'Poor William!' laughed Miss Mist sympathetically

and watched as he unlocked the door. She was wondering about asking him over to her attic for a mug of drinking chocolate, but was too shy for that too. Instead she murmured, 'Goodnight,' and drifted away.

Weeble entered his video room, switched on the light and surveyed the gleaming machines with a mixture of pride and dread—how he wished he was a bit more practical; he was sure to do everything wrong. Then he gasped—AH!—like that. This was because he'd seen someone crouching under a table.

'Wot are you doing in 'ere?' asked the man under the table.

'I—I'm the Head of Video,' explained Mr Weeble. 'I've taken over from Mrs Yapp.'

'Oh,' replied the stranger climbing out, 'that's all right then. Only there are a lot of funny people about. When you come in I got scared—that's how I come to be hiding under the table. All right?'

'Yes, of course,' replied Mr Weeble anxiously. He was a deeply polite person and he didn't want the stranger to feel he was unwanted.

'I'm here to see to the video machines,' the mysterious man replied. 'They are due for their service—they have to be serviced regular you understand.'

'Yes, of course, but. . . .' William Weeble's soft voice trickled to a standstill. He had been going to ask this helpful stranger why he was wearing a knitted mask over his head, but it seemed rather a personal thing to ask about, so he kept quiet.

'I 'spect you're wondrin' why I got this hood on me 'ead,' chuckled the stranger. 'It's 'cos I'm so ugly. I got a mutilated face—want to have a look?'

'N-no thank you. . . .'

'I weren't *born* ugly,' explained the stranger. 'When I was a nipper I was 'andsome. But I got kidnapped on account of my dad being a lord. Held to ransom I was!'

'Dear me!' exclaimed Mr Weeble. 'How awful. One reads about these things happening but one never really thinks about the terrible effect such an experience must have upon a little child.'

'It 'ad a terrible effect on me all right,' agreed the hooded helper. 'The villains wot kidnapped me cut off one of me ears and sent it to my dad to show they weren't larking about. Only they made the mistake of *washing* it first—so, of course, my dad, he said, "This ain't my boy's ear," he said. So they sends 'im the other one, an 'e says that one was too clean an 'all! So they sends 'im my little freckled nose all wrapped up in a paper hanky!'

'How terrible,' gasped William Weeble; his little, fat face was pale and he'd gone all trembly.

'Yes,' agreed the unfortunate stranger with a bitter sigh, 'I've 'ad a 'ard life!'

After that there was a pause. Mr Weeble couldn't

think of anything to say. He just stood there hoping the mutilated man wouldn't insist on taking his hood off to show him how hideous he was.

'Well, I must get on,' said the stranger eventually. 'Only I've got to load all these videos and stuff into the van.'

'What?'

'Yes, we works on 'em at home—see—in the workshop.'

'But I'm supposed to be recording all sorts of programmes!'

'That's all right,' explained the stranger, 'we'll do it for you. Just you give me a list.'

What a kind, helpful person that stranger was. No wonder Mr Weeble offered to carry the heavy machines to the van for him, because, as the stranger explained, 'I done my back in and can't hardly lift a cup of tea.'

There was another man in the driving seat of the van. A huge tank-like man, he nodded at Weeble in a friendly way.

'That's my brother,' the first man told Weeble.

'But he's wearing a hood as well.'

''Course he is.'

'But why?'

''Cos he's even more mutilated than wot I am.'

'You mean you were both kidnapped?'

'Not at the same time,' the stranger informed him. 'They done us one by one.'

Weeble looked at the gigantic hooded figure in the van.

'Yes, that's my big brother, that is,' explained the stranger softly. 'Lord Wapping.'

5

Killer Keast always arrived in his office early at the start of the school day. He believed many of his teachers were too nutty and soft to be able to deal with the modern brat unless he was on patrol all day, flashing his glare here and there terrifying people. That meant he had to arrive at school at about 7.30 to do his paper work. Headmasters have to do a lot of paper work—writing references and stuff like that. (As I expect you realise, references are for when kids leave school; universities and prisons write to their Headmasters asking what they are like.)

The Killer had just arrived at work on the morning after the videos had been taken away, and was sitting behind his desk writing his first reference of the day when there was a knock on his door.

Knock.

Knock.

'PETER PETERS,' wrote the Killer—he always ignored knocks for a minute or two to keep people in their place. 'PETER IS AN IDLE, HALF-WITTED WASTREL WHOSE ONLY TALENT IS SHOP LIFTING: HE SHOULD FEEL VERY MUCH AT HOME AT OXFORD. . . .'

KNOCK!!

KNOCK!!!

KNOCK!!!!

'Who the devil's that?'

'Me, sir,' answered a muffled voice.

'Well, come in; *open* the door—don't knock it down! Oh, it's you.'

'Yes, sir,' replied the caretaker who entered apprehensively. 'I'm sorry to disturb you only there's been a break-in; all the videos have been nicked!'

'See,' said the caretaker, 'they've left the window open.'

The Killer peered at the video-room window. 'Yes,' he replied. 'Well, I'll ring the police station.'

'Good morning!' cried a fresh little voice; it was Miss Mist skipping across the playground on her early morning prance. (Prancing is a sort of jogging; it's the way poetry teachers keep slim and beautiful.)

'It's *not* a good morning,' replied the Killer. 'All the video equipment has gone.'

'Oh, yes,' smiled the Head of Poetry brightly, 'some men with a van took them last night.'

'You saw them?'

'Yes.'

The Killer was not surprised. Years of dealing with art teachers and poetry teachers had made him very hard to surprise. 'Come with me to my office,' was all he said, 'you will have to talk to the police.'

A serious detective from the Serious Crime Squad

arrived to inspect the empty video room and interview Miss Mist. He had a lovely red nose, tastefully studded with black-heads. Miss Mist thought they made a very pretty pattern. He wore a detective-style mac and an ace-reporter-style hat which he took off and placed carefully on top of the pile of references on Killer Keast's desk before saying, 'Please sit down, Miss Mist.' There was a faint misty sound—which was Miss Mist saying 'thank you'. That was followed by a little creak as she sat on a chair.

'Now where were you last night when you saw these men taking the videos?'

'In the shrubbery.'

'What time would that be?'

'About eleven.'

'And you were in the shrubbery?'

'Yes, near the tennis courts near where the bee-hives are.'

'What were you doing there?'

This was a difficult question for poor little Miss Mist to answer. She had been doing three things:

1   She had been looking at the stars and thinking how many of them there were and how far away they were and how small she was and how Mr Weeble was like a star.

2   She had been thinking about the bees and how during the summer the shrubbery round the hives would be buzzing—and how Mr Weeble was like a

bee, always busy.

3   She had been thinking that maybe she should write a special Weeble-poem about how Mr Weeble was a bit like a star and a bit like a bee.

How exactly do you say all that to a serious policeman with egg on his tie?

'I-I was checking the hives,' she explained. 'We keep the beehives there. Beekeeping is an interest of mine. The school used to have a special little farm for some of the less academic teachers, but now they all have to do proper work and they have got rid of all the animals apart from the bees. I volunteered to be Head of Bees as well as Head of Poetry.'

The egg-stained sleuth made a note of this. 'So you were out by the beehives?'

'Yes.'

'And did anything unusual occur?'

'Yes, I saw a big van parked in the playground and a man was sitting in it with a tea-cosy over his head. Then I saw Mr Weeble carrying a very heavy television set. And another man with a tea-cosy on was talking to him.'

'What did Mr Weeble do with the television?'

'He put it in the van.'

'Then what did he do?'

'He went back to the video room and came back with an even heavier set.'

'And did you see him put that in the van too?'

'Yes.'

The egg-stained one smiled and made some notes. Then he looked up keenly. 'And this continued, did it? He kept loading the van with stuff?'

'Yes—he became most fatigued—the man with the tea-cosy didn't help at all! He just stood about! Then he got into the van with the other tea-cosy man and they drove away. Then Mr Weeble got into his car and. . . .'

'Drove after them?'

'Yes.'

'Thank you, Miss Mist. You have been most helpful!'

6

Whenever teachers get arrested for being burglars, their Headmasters keep quiet about it. If one of your teachers, for example, got done for robbing a bank or for being a cat burglar—or a dog burglar—you would probably never know. That teacher would just suddenly disappear and everyone would just think that he or she was ill.

It was the same at Shambles School; only Killer Keast and the other teachers knew that William Weeble had been arrested for being a video thief; the kids were not informed.

'Wuugh!'

'Wuugh!'

'Wuugh!'

The cheery sound of Twerpish laughter echoed about the rambling rooms of the Twerpery; the boys had just returned from school on the day after the video snatch. Micky was lying on the floor with his feet in the bread oven and his head cushioned comfortably on Hercules' tummy.

'Stop laughing!' squeaked the Flea.

'Wuugh!'

'Wuugh!'

'I'm serious,' she cried. 'I am on strike! That's why

there's no tea! That's why there'll be no breakfast!
That's why the house is in a mess and covered with
cobwebs! That's why there's a mountain of washing-
up in the sink! That's why you haven't any clean
clothes and your shirts haven't been ironed!'

'Wuugh!'

'Wuugh!'

The Flea went on strike from time to time and
whenever it happened the boys had to cook their
own meals. There'd be terrible burning smells and
clouds of smoke.

Sometimes the Flea went on strike in order to
serve them right for lolling about and not doing
anything to help except offer useful advice like, 'This
fish makes me feel sick!'

Sometimes she went on strike to toughen her boys
up so that they'd get used to living in a hard, mean
world.

But this time it was because she was fed up. 'I'm
fed up,' she explained, 'with everyone thinking I'm a
wonderful, zany, fun person. I'm going to show the
world I'm a rat!' She stalked up and down in a rat-like
way for a while before continuing: 'Do you know
what happened to me last night?'

The boys didn't answer. Even Hercules had learnt
that a good way to tease the Flea was to pretend you
weren't interested when she was bursting to tell you
something.

Kevin was the best at looking deeply uninterested.

He surveyed the Flea with his special, calm, slightly-scornful, deeply-bored look. Then he sighed.

The Flea paced about with rat-like tread thinking that she wouldn't be the first to weaken; those boys were secretly dying of curiosity; one of them would speak.

'What happened to you?' asked Hercules at last.

'I went to a meeting of the Shambles Art and Culture Committee. . . .'

'The what?' grinned Micky.

'It's to bring Art and Culture to the Shambles area.'

'What were *you* doing there?'

'What do you mean? I'm artistic and cultured, aren't I? Anyway I was specially asked to go. That little Miss Mist rang me. "Oh Mrs Twerp," she said, "we're looking for someone *dynamic* and *full of ideas!*" '

'Wuugh!'

'So I went along trying to look dynamic and full of ideas and there were all these people there with beards and glasses and Miss Mist was warbling on and on about this group she was in. . . .'

'Miss Mist—in a group?' gasped Kevin. Even he was surprised.

'Yes. She said it specialised in baroque music of the seventeenth century, so I said I didn't know there'd been any rock music in the seventeenth century and they all chortled and sniggered and steamed their glasses up, and Miss Mist said I was a

scream. Then they explained that Miss Mist's group played harpsichords and recorders and violas and whiffle-flutes and Miss Mist piped up: "I'm the whiffle-flute!"

'Then she said they needed someone *dynamic* and *well-organised* as bookings secretary to organise all their bookings—and they all looked at *me!* So I told them I wasn't dynamic or well-organised; I told them I was *lethargic* and *chaotic* and anyway I didn't have a *beard* or *glasses!*

'Then they all cheered and clapped and said what a *scream* I was and voted me in; so now I'm a whiffle-flautist's booking agent! And I said to myself as I walked home, *Flea,* I said, *you are a mug.* That's what I said. *You spend all your life running round after other people being dynamic and Flea-like. You should stop running round,* that was my advice to myself. And I have taken my own advice; from now on I'm going to *drift* about being *undynamic* and *rat-like.* It's the new policy. Don't call me Flea anymore, call me *Rat!*'

'Did anyone ring up for me this afternoon, Rat?' asked Micky.

'Possibly,' replied the rat-like Flea.

'Was it about the Perpetrators?'

'Maybe.'

As you may know, Micky Twerp was the lead singer of this hard rock band, 'The Perpetrators'. This group was Stage One of Micky's quest for fame and fortune. First he had called it 'The Perpetrators of the

Outrage' and the members of the group had gone about trying to look *hard* and *mean*. Unfortunately, however hard they tried, they still looked like the sort of boys that helped old ladies cross the road; so after a bit they dropped the 'Outrage' and became 'The Perpetrators'. They played in youth clubs and at parties—things like that. But Micky was always hoping that Alfie Wrench, the landlord of 'The Artful Snatcher', would ring up and book 'The Perpetrators'. 'The Artful Snatcher' was a really tough pub—full of hard cases—but they ran rock nights and hired good bands. To be booked by Alfie Wrench meant you were on the way up.

Of course, Micky and his group were too young even to go into the Snatcher, let alone play there. But he'd sent a demonstration tape to Alfie without mentioning that they were still at school; maybe he'd be in touch.

Even if they had been old enough, 'The Artful Snatcher' was not the sort of place for the kind of person that helped old ladies cross the road. Even when they were quietly listening, the yobs down at the Snatcher had that just-watch-it air of people looking for trouble. So it was just as well that when Micky went to the telephone table and looked at the jotter, he found these words scrawled by the Flea: *Church Assembly Rooms—tonight—8.00 pm—£20 + expenses.*

It was always a rush to get out for a gig, and the Flea's strike didn't help a bit. For one thing she refused to make anything for the boys to eat, and for another she refused to take them to the Assembly Rooms.

'I'm not running you about. One of the other parents can do it.'

'But Blister's dad is away, and the Boils haven't got a car!'

'Well, you'll have to walk.'

'How can Kevin walk there with his piano?'

'With difficulty!'

That proved to be true. It was very hard lugging that piano—even though it was only an electronic one. In the end 'The Perpetrators' had to tie all their stuff onto bikes and push them through the streets; it was especially tough on Kevin who was by far the youngest but with the heaviest instrument.

It was ten past eight when they arrived.

'Are you the musicians?' cried an anxious voice. 'Yes, of course you are! Thank goodness you've come; I was getting worried.' This anxious voice belonged to a stout lady with permed hair and pearls. She had stopped sounding anxious by the time she opened her mouth again—which wasn't very long: 'I say, it's *marvellous* you being able to come at such short notice—only the others have all gone down with 'flu, poor things!' She stopped gushing and paused politely for the boys to reply. Only they didn't, so she surged on: 'It is wonderful to see that you're all so *young!* It's a *very* musical audience tonight. I'm *sure* you'll find them appreciative. Professor *Smith* from the *Royal Academy* is here. We have all heard *so* much about your music; we are *really* looking *forward* to hearing you!'

Kevin looked keenly at the lady with the pearls; he'd heard about groupies; maybe that's what this lady was. Cor!

Back at the Twerpery little Hercules was sitting up in bed in his Spiderman pyjamas grinning at his mother. She was crumpled up in a heap at the foot of his bed giggling.

From far away, in the old billiard room, a weird honking could be heard. That was Rose; she was in there hooting and honking with laughter. Ever since Micky and Kevin had gone staggering off into the night, the Flea had been laughing. She'd laughed so much that Rose had come out of her room (the room she let from the Twerps—the old billiard room) and asked her what was up. It had been a long time before the Flea had been able to tell her, but she'd managed. After that Rose went hysterical too. It was eerie.

'Does this mean you're back to being Flea again— not Rat any more?' asked the little chap.

'No,' chortled the Flea. Then she curled up and *wept* with laughter.

On stage at the Assembly Rooms, Micky Twerp growled into the microphone. Growling and howling were a big part of the act. Audiences liked it; they often joined in—but not the lady with the pearls. She didn't seem to be entering into the spirit of things. And Professor Smith and the rest of them were managing to refrain from growling and howling too. It was weird. Deeply weird.

The Flea was still sniggering on the end of Hercules' bed when the door creaked open and Rose tumbled in with a happy smirk to say goodnight. 'I'm on duty all night,' she explained, 'sitting in the station with nothing to do—all because the Serious Crime Squad have arrested one of the video gang and he won't talk.'

'Won't talk?'

'No, Flea, he won't talk. He'll wail and blubber, but he won't tell them a thing. He's in the cells and that means the station has to be manned—or womanned—all night.'

But the Flea was not paying attention. She'd burst out giggling again. Tears were running down her cheeks. 'It was brilliant,' she gurgled, 'they all fell for it!'

'Yeh!' laughed Rose. 'Switching round those bookings was really rat-like!'

'I-I keep thinking about Miss Mist,' shrieked the Flea, 'down at "The Artful Snatcher"!'

I am very much afraid that Miss Mist's music had not

been received courteously by the yobs at 'The Artful Snatcher'. And her rustic smock had been singled out for comment.

7

The Flea was in bed when the boys got back to the Twerpery.

'Maybe we should wake her up with a water bomb,' suggested Kevin grimly. But her door was locked. There was a giggling sound from inside; a weak voice told them to go away and take their water bomb with them. The Flea seemed to be able to guess what was going on in her sons' heads; it was uncanny.

After a bit Micky began to see the funny side of things. A grin spread itself over his friendly face as he remembered the looks of horror on the unfriendly faces of the music lovers at the Assembly Rooms when he first started to growl at them. The two young Twerps returned down the stairs chortling to themselves. The Flea might be a menace, they agreed, but on the whole it was better having a Flea-type mum than an ordinary one. Ordinary mums were ordinary, the boys decided after deep thought, but the Flea made things happen. She was a mum with a mission, said Micky. A mission to perk people up.

An eerie bonging sound suddenly echoed through the hall, the front door bell. It was little Miss Mist; she was standing outside the Twerpery looking extra-twee because she was standing between two huge, muscular men with scars all over their heads.

'Come in,' said Micky politely. The two boys led the

way to the breakfast room, while Miss Mist explained the purpose of her visit. 'I fear your dear mother may have made a mistake,' she prattled, 'only she rang to say we had a booking at "The Artful Snatcher". She said that "The Artful Snatcher" was full of music lovers who specially liked baroque and we should go round there this evening at eight. There'd be a collection, she said, and as much beer as we could drink.

'Well, when we arrived a funny little man with skull tattoos on the backs of his hands met us and said that he'd heard a tape of us and thought we were great. Then we heard this rather frightening noise—like feeding time at the zoo—and this man said, "That's the fans," he said, "go in," he said, "and give it to 'em hot!"

'So we went out onto the stage—me in my rustic smock, Jasmin in her pantaloons and dear Cynthia with her Bo-Peep dress. But as soon as we stepped out onto the stage we were greeted with these terribly vulgar *raspberries!* They were all laughing and jeering and flicking beer mats at us. That's when these two gentlemen came to our rescue.'

'Yeh,' agreed the smaller of the two giants modestly. 'We just calmed things down a little. Only being so big we're respected, see? Also my views on violence are well known down the Snatcher; I hate violence—the lads know that. If I see people being violent I belt 'em. That's how I deal wiv it, see? Only being well known in the wrestling game the yobs is scared of us, see. So I gets up onto the stage, didn't I?'

'Yes, indeed he did,' cried Miss Mist eagerly. 'He suddenly climbed onto the stage and told them to *belt up*—such an *unusual* expression. "Belt up," he said, "or I'll do you!" Then everything went quiet,' continued Miss Mist. 'Only he said it wasn't quiet enough. He said they'd have to be a whole lot quieter. He said he didn't like to see ladies insulted by a load of pig-ignorant yobs!'

'That's right,' agreed the small giant. 'I told 'em I didn't like their attitude and my brother didn't like it neither. What they done was the sort of things what made my brother agitated. And if my brother gets agitated he can't answer for what might happen. That's what I told them yobs and they went so quiet they was 'ardly breathing.'

'Yes,' said Miss Mist, 'so we played our instruments and went through our programme of rustic tunes and the yobs were most attentive and appreciative and at the end this kind gentleman asked if he could borrow dear Cynthia's Little Bo-Peep bonnet and this other gentleman went round collecting money in it and his brother said that they were all to give generously—or they might regret it.'

By now the visitors were seated comfortably in the breakfast room; and the two big men were looking round approvingly.

'That's Terry Twerp,' said the bigger one pointing

at the poster of the boys' father which always hung in the breakfast room. 'I was a mate of Terry Twerp I was—when I was a nipper.'

'Yes,' explained the not-so-huge one. 'We was at the same school as Terry Twerp. We knowed him before he was famous.'

'Famous,' echoed the huge one.

'These boys are Terry Twerp's sons,' burbled Miss Mist. It was as if she was trying to impress the two men—just as they had been trying to impress her when they said they'd been at school with Terry Twerp.

''E was a pop star,' the big one explained—just in case the boys didn't know. ''E sang songs.'

'Yes,' said Micky.

''E 'ad lots of money but 'e spent it all,' said the slightly-less gigantic one shaking his head sadly.

'We know,' said Kevin.

''E's dead now,' said the big one.

There was silence.

Miss Mist thought she should say something to change the subject so she thought for a while, then she cried out: 'This has been such an eventful day. What with poor, dear William being arrested. Such a shock!'

'What 'appened?' asked the not-so-big one.

'He's been arrested for stealing videos,' yelped Miss Mist. 'He's down at the police station. It's so out of character. Such a kind dear man! It's terrible to think of him going to prison!' She began to cry. Little tears welled up in her big, brown eyes and tumbled down her sweet face.

There was another silence. Then the huge one spoke: 'Don't cry,' he said softly. 'I don't like to see a lady cry. He'll be all right—we'll bust him out!'

'Bust him out?' cried little Miss Mist.

'Yes—bust him out!'

8

Policewoman Rose Button sat behind the reception desk at Shambles Police Station and yawned. She was bored. There was nothing to do and no one to talk to.

To think, she thought to herself, that funny little fat teacher had been the leader of a most fiendish video gang—who'd have thought it! He seemed so wet and wimp-like; it only went to show how you could never tell what people were really like. And how sickening to think that such a deeply cunning villain had been so easy to catch. If the big-heads in the Serious Crime Squad hadn't been around, she might have nabbed him herself. As it was those half-witted creeps had got all the credit!

That was true, the members of the Serious Crime Squad had been going about looking extra-smug. They seemed to believe that it was their superior brain-power which had led to the arch-criminal's arrest instead of just a bit of luck. Still, Rose considered, there was still the rest of the gang to be rounded up, the two hooded men that the witness had seen; maybe *she* would be the one to track them down!

Ahem!

A polite cough aroused her. Two hooded men were standing in front of her. 'We've come to give ourselves up,' said the bigger one.

'We never wanted to be thieves,' said the other one.

'We wanted to be ballet dancers.'

'Yeh, ballet dancers.'

'My brother here was specially talented. . . .'

'Yeh, specially talented.'

'Only he has the strength for it, see? Ordinary men ballet dancers can only hold one ballerina up in the air at a time whereas he could hold up three or four. . . .'

'Yeh, three or four.'

'He could juggle wiv 'em!'

'Yeh, juggle wiv 'em.'

'He'd most likely be the most famous ballet dancer in the world by now if we hadn't been led into a life of crime by that smooth-talking villain Weeble.'

'Yeh, Weeble.'

'So we come down to give ourselves up.'

'Great!' chortled Rose. 'Follow me!'

'In here,' she smiled, unlocking a cell door and opening it wide.

'Thank you,' said the slightly smaller one artfully snatching the keys from her fist.

'After you!' growled the bigger one barging into her.

S L A M ! That was the cell door slamming.

Rose was all by herself again.

Kevin never showed that he was surprised by anything. He had not shown surprise earlier that evening when Professor Smith had refused to howl; he had shown no surprise when most of the audience

had walked out; he had not been surprised when it was revealed that those who had remained were all deaf. The rest of the Perpetrators had been amazed: 'What are they doing here if they're all deaf?' they had shrieked. 'Enjoying the music,' the lady with the pearls had replied coldly.

Yes, amazement, wonder, and a deep sense of the mystery of life could be seen on the faces of the other Perpetrators—but not on Kevin's; his expression had remained calm. It is true that a ghostly smile like an upturned new moon had appeared on his lips when he first noted the age and appearance of the audience. That smile had grown less ghostly and more grin-like as the evening wore on, but he had not looked surprised.

Some people say that it is impossible to surprise Kevin Twerp but they are wrong. William Weeble surprised him.

You may not believe this—but when Kevin burst into Micky's attic after answering the door, he was actually flustered. Yes: he was worried and anxious and bewildered and amazed; he wanted to bring his big brother in on things as soon as possible.

'Weeble's here!' he yelped.

'Weeble?'

'The front bell rang and it was Weeble. It's *him* they bust out!'

'What!'

'Yes. They bust him out and told him to come here!'

Micky shot out of bed and headed downstairs. Busting people out of jail was frowned on by the police. And helping busters out once they have busted out is a serious crime.

What should he do?

Tell him to clear off?

Wake the Flea?

Ring Miss Mist?

What?

Micky Twerp who usually saw the funny side of things, took a long time before he saw the funny side of busting out.

'Look, sir, you can't stay here. A policewoman lives in this house. She could arrive any minute!'

Mr Weeble leapt out of his chair and listened desperately for policewomen, but all he heard was a clock ticking calmly on the breakfast room wall. Then he heard young Micky Twerp's earnest voice speaking urgently: 'If you were caught and it looked as if we'd been hiding you, my mother could get thrown into jail herself.' Micky stood there feeling sensible. He'd decided *not* to wake the Flea; he and Kevin were probably too young to get into serious trouble for helping a criminal on the run, but the Flea would be arrested; the less she knew about it, the better.

'I-I'm sorry,' stammered the woeful Weeble. 'Only terrible things keep happening to me. I get arrested for no reason and people scream at me all day about videos and then I'm left all alone in a cell that smells like a school toilet. There were no sheets on the bed or anything—not even a glass for my teeth. I had to put them under the bed. . . .in fact they're still there— do you think it would be unwise to go back for them?'

'Yes,' advised Micky. 'It would be unwise.'

'Oh dear!' sighed the King of Crime.

Micky and Kevin glanced at each other with a *what-shall-we-do* look.

You must remember that they did not actually know that Weeble was innocent; they kept thinking that maybe they should ring the police, but the poor little chap looked so sad and crumpled—it was hard to imagine that he was a thief.

There was a flash of light; a car was coming up the drive.

'That'll be Rose,' said Micky quietly. 'Kevin go and head her off—keep her talking. I'll help Mr Weeble get clear.'

Moonlight sifted into the eerie hall of the Twerpery making it spooky. Something ghostly came gliding down the stairs.

'Kevin,' it hissed, 'what are you doing wandering about? It's two o'clock in the morning! What's going on?' Fortunately the Flea did not have time to receive an answer; there were unlocking noises; the front door rocketed open; something big and blob-like bounded in clicking at the light switch and muttering when nothing happened. The hall bulb had gone and

Micky had forgotten to change it.

'Rose, is that you?' squeaked the Flea.

'Yes it is,' answered the big blob.

'Has everyone gone mad?' squeaked the Flea.

'Yes,' replied Rose grimly, 'especially the Serious Crime Squad!'

'Kevin,' snapped his mother, 'who is in the breakfast room?'

'Micky.'

'Who's he talking to?'

'Himself.'

The Flea flounced down into the hall and surged towards the breakfast room. Rose followed muttering.

Micky was lolling on a bean bag reading one of Hercules' comics; the comic was upside down but that did not seem to stop him laughing: 'Wuugh! Wuugh! Wuugh!'

'Why are you and Kevin trying to keep me awake all night?' the Flea demanded to know. 'If I don't get my beauty sleep I shall get wrinkles and bags under my eyes. You will look at me in the morning and shudder! *Who's she?* you'll say. *Who's that shrivelled old crone?*'

'Wuugh!'

'And what are *you* doing here?' cried the Flea turning on the muttering Rose. 'You're supposed to be hard at work guarding a dangerous criminal, not barging about the house like a rhinoceros on roller-skates!'

'He's been bust out,' replied Rose simply. 'His gang burst in and surrounded me! There was nothing I could do! It wasn't my fault!'

There was more silence. Then Rose spoke again; her voice was husky because of all the screaming she'd had to do. 'But I have been *blamed,*' she announced huskily. 'The Serious Crime Squad want me sacked!'

'Sacked, Rose?'

'Yes, Flea. Sacked! There's only one way out—I've got to track down that fiend Weeble before they do! It's my only chance!'

9

As the Twerpery finally settled down for the night, a lonely figure could be observed walking along the road that flanked the jungle—as the Twerpery garden was called; Killer Keast was out for a moonlight walk.

You see, the Killer had not always been wild and savage. There had been a time, not long before, when he had been mild and kitten-like. Instead of yelling and snarling, he had gone about patting children on the head and telling the teachers not to get cross.

It had been love that had made the Killer kitten-like; it had seeped into his soul and made him mild. Yes—he had been deeply in love with a larger-than-average policewoman and love had made him happy until the day that he had asked her to marry him. He had looked up at her in the soft romantic candlelight and thought how lovely she was. 'Will you marry me, my darling?' he had asked tremblingly. 'I'm sorry,' she had answered, taking his hand, 'but much as I respect and admire you, I could never marry a man who so closely resembled an elk—it would not be fair on the children.' Then she had squeezed his hand until something snapped. The Killer had been in his Grade Z mood ever since.

He could not sleep at night for thinking of the lovely policewoman. Often he would walk about the empty streets. Always he would end up by the Twerpery and gaze into its jungle with mournful eyes. That's what happened on the night of the bust out; he gazed with mournful eyes at a chunk of jungle—then, with a jump of surprise, he realised that the chunk of jungle was gazing back!

'Who's there?' he growled menacingly. The chunk of jungle did not reply. Branches swayed. Then there was silence.

It had been an eerie experience for the Killer; there had been something other-worldly about that pair of blinking eyes. Next morning, sitting in his office, he shuddered as he remembered them.

'Sir! Sir!' His door flew open and a boy burst in.

'Yes, Smith, what is it?'

'There's this huge tree in the boys' toilets, sir! Growing up out of one of the loos!'

'What are you talking about?' snarled the Killer.

'I just went in there and there were these branches coming out of one of the cubicles. It must have grown up overnight, sir, like in *Day of the Triffids!* Maybe some special acorn is responsible, sir. Maybe someone ate one—it could have been muesli, sir. Then they went into the boys' toilets, sir and. . . .'

'Yes, Smith. I take your point.'

The tree had just left when the Headmaster arrived in the boys' toilets. 'It just pulled the chain and went out,' explained a trembling First Year, 'without washing its hand.'

'Did it have a hand?'

57

'Yes, sir. Just one. It was green.'

The Killer glared at the two boys. Then he shuddered again for he remembered the eerie experience of the blinking eyes.

'Go back to your classrooms,' he said sternly. 'Tell no one about what you have seen.'

'Yes, sir.'

At break the Killer summoned all his teachers and told them not to panic.

'We're not panicking,' replied Jock McStrapp, the Head of PE.

'What is there to panic about?' asked Miss Fitt, Head of Hockey. 'The fourth year yobs aren't fighting again, are they?'

'No,' replied the Head.

'It's not the third year girls, is it?' cried Miss Mist. 'They haven't all gone hysterical again, have they?'

'Not as far as I know,' replied the Killer. 'But it is difficult to tell.'

'Well what's there to panic about?' Miss Fitt again demanded to know. Like all PE teachers, she got directly to the point.

'The school appears to have been invaded by an alien life form,' replied the Headmaster gravely. 'Two boys reported seeing it in the boys' toilets, and I myself saw something odd last night in the Twerps' garden.'

'A Twerp?' suggested Jock McStrapp helpfully. 'They are all odd.'

'This was not a Twerp,' announced the Killer, 'this was a *botanical* freak—not a human one.'

'But where is it now?' asked little Miss Mist anxiously.

'I don't know,' replied the Head. 'Shortly before break one of the groundsmen reported seeing a tree in the middle of a hockey pitch. . . .'

'That couldn't have been there yesterday,' gurgled Miss Mist, 'or the girls would have noticed!'

'Not necessarily,' said Miss Fitt.

'As I was saying,' growled the Killer stern'y, 'one of the groundsmen reported seeing a tree in the middle of a hockey pitch jumping up and down.'

'Who was jumping up and down,' croaked Mr Bilge, the Head of Biology, 'the groundsman or the tree?'

'The tree!'

'Most unusual,' Mr Bilge informed them, drawing upon a lifetime's experience.

'It is also unusual to see a groundsman jumping up and down,' squeaked the Head of Poetry.

'The groundsman did *not* jump up and down,' replied the Head. 'He ran to my office to inform me about the jumping tree. Then he took me to the place where he had seen it jumping, but it had gone.'

There was an excited buzz; not since the arrest of the Head of Video for burglary had the staff at Shambles School buzzed so excitedly.

'I have rung Kew Gardens and Whipsnade Zoo,'

announced the Headmaster coolly. 'And the police will be here shortly.'

'Is it a crime to jump up and down?' asked Miss Mist anxiously. 'Only I jump up and down quite a lot!'

'The police have to be informed about this possibly deadly peril,' explained the Head. 'The fire brigade will also be here—as soon as they find their missing wheel—so, as I said before, there is no need to panic. Just teach your classes in the normal way and if the children see anything unusual distract their attention.'

'How?' croaked the Head of Biology.

But the Killer ignored him; the bell was clanging; break was over.

Little Miss Mist came tripping into Kevin's class clutching her special poetry book, *Romantic Verses for Tough Schools*. She looked jumpy and kept glancing out of the window at the hockey and football fields.

'We will continue where we left off,' she announced tremulously. 'Open your books at page 96—"Ode to a Dying Ferret".'

Then, without pausing, she pitched straight in using her special poetry-reading voice:

> *O ferret curled up in your straw*
> *Soon you'll be gone and we no more*
> *Will hear your tinkling little bell*
> *Nor sniff your pungent ferret smell.*

'Now,' she said, wiping her eyes with a paper hanky, 'who can tell me what this poem is about?'

The children's deeply blank faces remained deeply blank.

'Well,' continued Miss Mist, 'an animal is mentioned in this poem. What sort of animal is it—Kevin?'

'Sick.'

'Yes. That is certainly true. But what I meant was. . . .'

'Ahhh!!!'

'Tracey! What's the matter?'

'Miss! Miss! Look out of the window, Miss!' yelled Masher Smith. 'It's the walking tree!'

The children proved very difficult to distract. By the time the fire engine appeared the whole school was out on the playing fields; fourth year yobs bravely leapt at bushes and shrubs; third year girls screamed; teachers rushed about roaring.

William Weeble stood by the beehives and hoped the bees wouldn't mind. He stood silent and still; from far away he could hear the screams of third year girls and a crash. It was only the fire engine knocking down the cricket pavilion, but Weeble wasn't to know that. To him those screams and that crash sounded sinister. Thank God everyone was searching round the playing fields and none of them knew where he was.

Knock.

Knock.

Good grief. Someone was knocking on his trunk.

61

'Are you all right in there, sir?' asked a boy's voice. Weeble felt it best to keep his mouth shut.

'It's all right, sir, it's only me—Kevin Twerp. There's no one else, sir.'

'Kevin Twerp?'

'Yes, sir. Are you okay, sir?'

'No, I'm not,' wailed Weeble. 'I'm tired and cold and hungry and everybody's out hunting for me. This was your brother's idea,' complained the ungrateful Weeble. 'He said it was a wonderful disguise! He said I could live in it for weeks and no one would suspect!'

'Well,' retorted Kevin loyally, 'you shouldn't have gone walking about—people naturally get suspicious when a little tree goes skipping past!'

The tree muttered and stuttered and shook its leaves until, suddenly, it froze. A motorbike was approaching.

'It's okay, it's only me!' called the cheery voice of Micky Twerp.

The tree muttered again—something about the Twerp family which they could not hear. Micky approached it and put his lips close to where he'd worked out Weeble's ears were.

'There'll have to be a change of plan,' Micky hissed. 'You'll have to get out of the tree-suit, sir, and borrow this bike, sir, and go out the back gates, sir. Only they think you're an alien life form, sir. And Mr McStrapp's gone to get his chainsaw. . . .'

The tree leapt up. It wriggled and shook. 'I'm

stuck!' it shrieked.

'Think about the chainsaw!' cried Kevin. 'Try harder, sir!'

That's when the tree leapt onto the motorbike. It was a very elegant, white motorbike, tastefully decorated with the word POLICE, and that plucky little tree jumped right onto it.

Vroom.

Vroom.

Vroom.

Weeble shot forward—which was a mistake. Yes—knocking down beehives is always a mistake—for when a cloud of mad bees are coming at you, you act first and think afterwards. Mr Weeble's idea of action was to pick up the bike, start it up again, and travel as far and as fast as possible.

The two young Twerps had very much the same idea; as the bike came upright they both piled onto the pillion pulling their sweaters over their heads.

'Go, sir! Go!' screamed Micky.

Angry bees were swarming over them; some stayed on their heads and shoulders madly trying to sting even when they were going fast.

'They're still after us!' screamed Kevin.

Weeble churned at the throttle with his little green fist.

'We're being chased, sir,' yelled Micky. 'It's Mr Keast, sir, and some men, sir. I think they are from Whipsnade Zoo, sir!'

Weeble went pale beneath his bark.

'Faster!' yelled Micky. 'Faster!'

It is difficult riding a motorbike with two boys on the pillion—especially if you have only one little green hand, can't move your legs easily, and your eye-holes aren't very big. But when Killer Keast is on your tail—you ride!

'The fire engine, sir,' one of the boys was screaming. 'It's stuck under the rugby posts, sir! But there's a lot of fourth year yobs, sir—on bikes, sir—and Mr McStrapp, sir, with his chainsaw, sir. . . .'

V R O O M ! ! !

'He's on top of the mini-bus, sir. Miss Fitt's driving it, sir. And Miss Mist's in there, sir. . . .'

'Miss Mist?' wailed Weeble.

'Yes, sir, Miss Mist, sir—Head of Poetry, sir, and Bees, sir. She's in the mini-bus, sir, in her beekeeper's hat, sir, in case of alien killer bees, sir! From Outer Space, sir, like they think you're from, sir!'

But the Feeble Weeble did not answer. Instead he steered his machine out of the school gates and onto the open road.

10

The members of the Townswomen's Guild are, as you know, rough, tough, and dangerous. If you get them mad, they fling things at you. I'm sorry to say that Mr William Weeble—usually such a mild-mannered man—did something to upset them. Actually it was their produce stall he upset; half a ton of homemade jam, two hundred fairy-cakes, a crate of eggs, and nine jars of prune and apricot chutney hit the street at once. But not the plum nut flan. That hit William Weeble—or rather his eye-holes. After that they were riding blind.

Plum nut flan is nutty, rich, and has a hint of ginger. You would have thought that Kevin Twerp would have been most grateful when the Townswomen threw one at him too. But he was not. Nor did he like the attitude of the china-stall lady; while the coster-mongers with their loud voices, keen aim, and ready supply of potatoes made him feel unwanted. You see, a tree riding blind through Shambles Street Market tends to irritate stallholders. People say things like, 'Is that a poplar tree that's just demolished the china stall?' And other people reply, 'Not at all. It is an unpoplar tree!'

'Quick!' Micky screamed at Kevin. 'Jump!'

Micky's decision was wise. This can be proved by the fact that, seconds after they jumped, Weeble

crashed. He was okay in his tree-suit—but the boys wouldn't have been. Even if the crash had not injured them, the falling videos could have killed them. Yes, thousands of pounds worth of heavy video equipment crashed and shattered. The two stallholders emerged from the wreckage—huge and furious.

'Now you've done it!' yelled the slightly smaller one. 'You've gone and made my brother agitated! An' when 'e's agitated 'e can't answer for what might 'appen!'

That's when the bees caught up.

Hercules Twerp was suffering from a most mysterious disease. It had struck him in the morning at breakfast time. 'Ow! Eeeh! I've got pains—in my tummy! And I've got a headache!' he had wailed to his worried mother.

'Stay in bed,' she had ordered firmly.

Then at about 9.00 am—PING—that mysterious disease disappeared. The little chap had managed to eat a few morsels of bacon and egg, fried bread, toast and jam, rice crispies, chocolate cake, a bag of sweeties, a banana and an apple or two.

'I'm feeling a little better,' the plucky lad managed to gasp, 'can I go swimming?'

An ordinary-type mum would have had a fit at this point—perhaps bitten the boy's ear—but the Flea just threw a wet dish cloth at him. Luckily it landed smack on his face, which put her in a good mood. 'Oh, all right you fiend,' she laughed. 'Rose!' she yelled. 'We're going swimming—wanna come?'

That's how Rose got to come with them; she was a demon swimmer with lots of cups and medals and, as the Flea had pointed out, a good swim would cheer her up and do her good and stop her mooning about the house like a sick bison.

There were two swimming baths to choose from in the Shambles area: the boring one and the one with the wave-machine and the super-slide. Guess which Hercules voted for?

A good thing about the one with the super-slide and the wave-machine was that the Shambles Market was right outside, so the Flea was able to do her shopping. She had finished before Weeble and the boys arrived so the market had been its usual, boring self while she'd been padding round it.

By the time the tree crashed into the video stall, the Flea was upstairs on the balcony of the pool. There were plastic tables up there and lots of greenery coming out of pots; you could sip coffee at the plastic tables and maybe munch a chocolate biscuit while you watched the swimmers in the pool far below.

'Mum! Mum!' screamed Hercules waving up at her. Flea waved back. This was nice, she thought; this was calm and peaceful. She didn't even have to keep an eye on Hercules because Rose was in the pool splashing about in the waves like a happy hippo.

Mums like being calm and peaceful. I expect you have noticed this about your own dear mother; they never really appreciate having frogs put down their wellies or the many other attempts that thoughtful children make to liven up their boring lives. Even the Flea, who was (as we know) a mum with a mission, liked being calm and peaceful when she had a chance.

She gazed about calmly and peacefully. Then peacefully and calmly, she fished about in her special Flea-bag and took out Kevin's personal stereo which she'd sort of borrowed from him without asking the way that mums do. You see she had this deeply calm and peaceful tape that Terry Twerp had recorded once when he had been feeling calm and peaceful. It was called 'Beautiful Eyes' and the Flea stuck the headphones on her ears, closed her eyes and listened. She'd been the one with the beautiful eyes, of course, so it was a pity she closed them. Especially as she missed seeing Kevin and Micky arrive.

Yes, the glass door marked EXIT flew open and two frantic boys with their sweaters still pulled over their heads burst in. They seemed most anxious to get into the water.

It was the bees, you see. There were about a dozen of them stuck to Kevin's head. Sometimes one of their stings would make contact with a bit of him—like an ear—and he'd go, 'Ah!'

Splash!

That was Kevin leaping in.

Splash!

That was Micky. Hercules was pleased to see them, but critical: 'You've still got your clothes on,' he pointed out.

'A tree!' squawked the little lad. 'A tree sliding down the super-slide!'

This was true; the alien life form—surrounded by the swarm of killer bees—was on the slide.

Here is a word of warning. If you are stuck in a tree-suit, *don't* go down a super-slide. If you think about it coolly you will see why: you can't swim in a tree-suit. But Weeble was not thinking coolly. The impact of the crash had knocked the flan out of the eye-holes; he'd seen the enraged giants emerging from the wreckage like two incredible Hulks. He'd heard them snarling—felt the big one's boot. Only the bees had saved him.

Those bees blamed the Weeble-tree for smashing up their hive. *Sting the Weeble*—that was their motto. *Go up inside his trousers and sting whatever you find up there:* that was the buzz they were buzzing. *And sting anyone else who's handy!* That was another slogan.

Yes, troops of bees had marched up inside Weeble's trousers, stinging as they went—and they went a long way! Bees had attacked the heads and crumpled ears of the video thieves—until they'd put their hoods on. Bees had attacked Kevin and Micky, Killer Keast, third year girls, fourth year yobs—

70

everyone apart from Miss Mist in her beekeeping hat.

'The pool! The pool!' the Headmaster had roared. 'Immerse yourselves! These are killer bees! They have come out of that extra-terrestial thing!'

Then there had been another buzzing: a sinister, terrible buzz—the buzz of a chainsaw. That's when Weeble had gone crazy. 'Water!' he'd warbled. 'Get out of the way! Water! Water!'

''Ere,' hissed the smaller giant as he had chased the tree into the swimming pool. 'I recognise that voice! That's not no extra-terrestial thing! That's an extra-terrestial Weeble!'

'Yeh,' grunted the big brother, 'Weeble!'

'Let's get 'im!' hissed the slightly smaller one.

'Yeh! Get 'im!'

If you are heavy and coated in fibre-glass, you go really, really fast on a super-slide: unless you get stuck. Then you stop. Suddenly.

That is what happened to William Weeble. He was flying nimbly down the slide when—THWOCK—the tree stopped and he went on without it.

Yes! The tree had got stuck, but Weeble had finally got unstuck. One minute he was in that ghastly tree-suit being stung on the bum and the next—splash!—he was in the pool alongside everyone else.

Weeble's happy head bobbed up and down. He wore a cheery smile. Bliss—his bum was bee-less. It's true a larger-than-average female had that happy head in an arm-lock, but she was probably just trying

71

to save his life.

A familiar voice could be heard roaring above the jabbering crowd in the pool. It was the Head.

'Stay in the water,' he was telling everybody. 'They are alien bees brought to this planet by that *thing!*' He pointed to the tree—which was still sitting calmly on the super-slide.

The awe-struck brats of Shambles School shuddered. It was eerie to be in the same building as an alien life form. Two huge, hooded men were slithering down the super-slide towards the *thing*.

'Who are they, sir?' shrieked a third year girl excitedly.

'It must be the SAS,' replied the Headmaster. 'Keep calm everyone—we'll soon be okay!'

'He's *gorn!*' growled the largest of the hooded figures examining the extra-terrestial tree. 'Where's he gorn then? WHERE'S WEEBLE ?'

'He's down here!' roared Rose. 'I've got him!'

The giant in the hood glared down at the crowded pool. At last he saw what he was looking for and began to yell: 'You 'orrible little Weeble! What did you smash up our stuff for? We was the ones what bust you out!'

'Yes,' yelped Weeble, 'and you were the ones that stole the stuff in the first place!'

'EXACTLY!' replied the big one emphatically. '*We* was the ones that nicked the stuff, so what right did *you* 'ave to come and smash it?'

·'That's right,' roared the slightly smaller one. 'It wasn't you what went to the trouble of nicking it! It wasn't you what took the risks! *You* never nicked none of it!'

'Yeh,' agreed the bigger one. 'So now we're gonna smash you!'

'I-I didn't mean to crash into your stall!' cried Weeble.

'It wasn't his fault!' yelled Micky Twerp. 'It was the Townswomen's Guild!'

'Yeh,' agreed Kevin. 'They threw that cake at him!'

'Flan,' corrected Weeble. 'It was a flan. But the Twerp boys are, alas, correct. Hooligan conduct on the part of the ladies from the Townswomen's Guild was indeed responsible for my accident.'

'Ladies?' asked the big giant, shaking his hooded head incredulously.

'Yes.'

'Well,' he sighed, 'if it was *ladies*, that's different. I never hit a lady—not even when I'm agitated!'

The video thieves sat silent for a while sadly considering the disgraceful conduct of the Townswomen's Guild. Then, grabbing the empty tree, they pulled it back to the top of the slide, and slowly descended the stairs.

'We're keeping this!' roared the slightly smaller one. 'It might come in useful!'

Out they went through the glass exit doors— followed by hundreds of eyes and the swarm of killer bees.

In the deep end the larger-than-average lady's arm-lock loosened.

Weeble found himself bobbing by himself. But not for long. Another pair of arms embraced him, a pair of slender poetic arms. Someone wrapped up in a net was trying to kiss him.

The Flea had a most relaxing morning. It's true that her coffee had gone cold by the time she woke up but so what?

She took her earphones off and, with a yawn, glanced down at the pool; only Hercules was in there bobbing happily up and down in his armbands. Rose must have had enough.

'Go and get changed!' she called.

'Okay.'

Yes, thought the Flea to herself. Just what I needed after being kept awake half the night—a little peace and quiet!

11

'They were practically stung to death,' honked Rose cheerfully.

'What, the video thieves?' asked Kevin calmly.

'No—not them—the real villains. The Serious Crime Squad!'

'Wuugh! Wuugh!'

'How come?' asked the Flea from her bean bag.

'They were out in the market sifting through the smashed videos when the brothers appeared with that wretched tree. So, being thick, they said, "That's *our* tree," they said. "Right," said the thieves, "you can have it back," and they picked it up and rammed it on top of one of them—the egg-stained one! So he got stung even more than Weeble 'cos he was so dim he ran all the way back to the police station. And all the other coppers were in there laughing at them and saying have you re-captured Weeble yet and so they got stung too!'

'What all of them?'

'Yeh. Serves 'em right. Then I came in with Weeble tucked under my arm. "Here he is," I said, "the King of Crime!" Only they couldn't see him because of all the smoke.'

'Smoke, Rose?'

'Yes, Flea, smoke. They were burning old rags to get rid of the bees—see? So I told them Weeble was innocent and there were hundreds of witnesses and could he have his teeth back please!'

'And I was with them too,' said a sweet melodious voice. 'And as soon as we located William's teeth he gave me the most lovely smile. .

'Wuugh!'

'. . .then he took me by the hand and led me away from the police station because it was a bit crowded in there—especially when the fire engine arrived. We went and sat down—at least I did, William preferred to remain standing. And he asked me to become *Mrs Weeble* and I-I said YES!'

The wedding reception was at a big hotel. Hercules got lost. Yes. Well it can easily happen. He found himself in the room where all the presents were on display. Two very large men with bushy white beards were in there putting the presents into a sack.

'Who are you?' asked the little chap.

'I'm Father Christmas,' explained the slightly smaller one, 'and this is one of my gnomes!'

'Gnomes are small!' said Hercules.

'Most of them are,' agreed Father Christmas, 'but not this one—this one's deformed.'

'For Christmas I want a BMX and a puppy and—and another puppy and a watch please,' requested Hercules politely.

'Okay,' said Father Christmas, 'so long as you

are good.'

'Yeh, good,' echoed the gnome.

'Only you shouldn't tell no one you seen us.'

'Why not?'

''Cos my gnome is shy.'

'Yeh—shy.'

''E's shy on account of being so big. People looks at 'im and passes remarks and 'e don't like it.'

'Okay,' said little Hercules. 'I won't tell them.'

Father Christmas and the gnome continued with their festive task and young Hercules Twerp drifted back to the party.

'I wonder why they were putting things *into* the sack instead of taking things *out* of it,' pondered the infant Twerp. The more he puzzled over this problem the more uneasy the little chap felt.

There were lots of tough grown-ups at the party—people like Killer Keast and Mr McStrapp. Maybe he should tell them. But what if they laughed at the gnome—or passed remarks? Then he saw Rose—Rose wouldn't laugh at a gnome just because he was deformed. After all she was deformed herself. No, Rose would be tactful. He'd tell Rose about it—she'd know what to do. And she did!

A Twerp Mystery

THE HEADMASTER WENT SPLAT!

David Tinkler

'Kevin Twerp,' hissed Killer Keast, the ferocious headmaster of Shambles School, 'I want to see you in my room immediately.'

Suddenly, it seemed to go cold. The light went dim. There was a gasp from the children and the teachers shivered. Kevin felt faint and his mouth went dry.

Kevin Twerp's life hasn't been easy; pop-singing dad killed in an air crash, Mum — Nitty Norah the Hair Explorer — driven out to work as a school nurse. And, looming, like a dark shadow, Killer Keast.

But, with the help of WPC Rose Button, lodger and All-England Mud Wallowing Champion, things *will* change . . . !

KNIGHT BOOKS